CW00863992

VOLUME 1

Tales of Nogion

D.L. MORGAN

authorHOUSE

AuthorHouse™ UK
1663 Liberty Drive
Bloomington, IN 47403 USA
www.authorhouse.co.uk
Phone: UK TFN: 0800 0148641 (Toll Free inside the UK)
*   UK Local: (02) 0369 56322 (+44 20 3695 6322 from outside the UK)*

Published by AuthorHouse   12/06/2021

ISBN: 978-1-6655-9083-9 (sc)
ISBN: 978-1-6655-9084-6 (hc)
ISBN: 978-1-6655-9085-3 (e)

Print information available on the last page.

This book is printed on acid-free paper.

"Since it is so likely that (children) will meet cruel enemies, let them at least have heard of brave knights and heroic courage. Otherwise you are making their destiny not brighter but darker."

— C.S. Lewis

Praise for *Tales of Nogion* (Volume 1)

Some of my greatest revelations from God's Word and through nature in relation to my communication with Him have come through the wisdom of a child. My granddaughter was so upset when she discovered I was sixty-five years old that she developed a plan to make me thirty years old again.

The secret was a sprinkle of 'fairy dust' the tooth fairy had left under her pillow. 'Bampi,' she said with wide eyes full of wonder, 'I will throw this fairy dust on you, and you will become thirty years old again!' And so it happened, SHAZAM, in one moment of wonder, in that little five-year-old's eyes, I became thirty years old again. She was so convinced of this that a year later, I received a birthday card from her wishing me a happy thirty-first birthday. That day, I was reminded of a verse in the Bible where Jesus said, 'Unless you become like a child, you can never really understand what my kingdom is all about.'

Dave's stories and poems reminded me of that experience with my granddaughter; and reading his stories and poems reminded me again that some of the greatest lessons we can learn about ourselves, God, and others are through the eyes of a child.

Although his book is designed for children, it's a necessary read for all of us.

I pray these stories and poems will release a sense of childlike wonder in all who read or hear them.

—Ray Bevan, pastor and author of *Prepared for Greatness, Journey to the Centre of Your Heart, Grace Shouts Louder,* and *Grace*

These short stories and rhymes are the perfect recipe for capturing the imagination and creativity of all children being read to, and indeed independent readers. The illustrations are suitable for all ages. The tales have the right amount of content to keep the reader's interest. They are humorous and at times quite mischievous but always show the reader that making the right choices delivers the best outcome.

—Shelia New, retired primary school teacher

Being a primary school teacher for the past thirteen years and having an avid interest in developing children's reading skills, I am honoured to have been asked to write an endorsement for this wonderful book written by my friend, and pastor of my church, David Morgan.

David is warm-hearted, kind, and one of the most thoughtful people I know. He is a teacher to many, a friend to all, and inspires children with his creative imagination.

This book features a central theme of imagination, consisting of a number of amusing, exciting, and thrilling characters. As I read the short stories and poems, I can imagine the excitement in the faces of a class of children, having to bring to life the fictional characters. In the same way, I saw the excitement in my son's face when he read about the warty skin and smelly breath of the Gob-O-lins, and the Grotchit who was trumpeting from his yellow nose! Engaging with fantasy can really stimulate creativity and boost vocabulary within children.

Aside from the fascinating characters, the principal factor of this book is the underlying message that is conveyed. It's vital that children learn and understand that things are not always as they seem on the outside, and that we shouldn't judge others on their outward appearance only. This book teaches children about empathy, kindness, and compassion for others—extremely important lessons that can be taught from a young age.

This is a book that is appealing and enticing to children on many levels. However, it includes a message for everyone, whatever your age.

—Rhian White, primary school teacher

Dave has a way of writing that will enable people from many differing backgrounds to envisage the most vivid of pictures in their imaginations. He manages to draw the reader into various worlds filled with colourful, strange, lovable, and magical characters whilst taking them on a journey that highlights the importance of having good Christian faith–based moral values and ethics that any parent would be proud to instil in their child. This is a must-read for those who enjoy being transported into a plethora of fantasy, frivolity, fun, and fiction, all compiled in one very tasty, easy-to-digest meal. I highly recommend it.

—Stephen Philip Boalch, pastor

It is no mean feat to write a book and an even greater challenge to write one that resonates with the curious minds of children and adults alike. *Tales of Nogion* does just that. It takes us back as adults to the magical days of our youth when everything was possible and the 'baddies' would never win! It further carries unspoken messages for the young mind—that it's not okay to trick others or plot the demise of the seemingly vulnerable. It gives hope of redemption and beckons us into a world where everything is possible … if only for a while.

I applaud Dave for these very clever nuances pervading *Tales of Nogion*, and I cannot wait for more of his published works.

—Bernie Davies, international number-one bestselling author and TEDx speaker

CONTENTS

CHAPTER 1

The Naughty Leprechaun

T MAY HAVE BEEN YESTERDAY. IT MAY HAVE BEEN A LONG time ago. But there once was a Leprechaun called Hamish Shamus Finnegan McGee, and he was a very naughty Leprechaun.

He had not always been 'very' naughty—just a bit to start with. Playing tricks on folk, telling tall tales, and being a bit greedy were normal kinds of naughtiness for Leprechauns, but McGee became naughtier than most.

Leprechauns are very good at making and fixing shoes and boots, and make a good living from it too! They work with their little hands and add a little magic to make the best footwear in the world. But Mr McGee was a cheat! He thought to himself, *Why work so hard and make one pair of shoes for a little money when I can make lots of shoes for a lot of money?*

So, Mr McGee opened a factory and filled it with Goblins to work for him instead! This was very naughty indeed and not allowed by the Leprechaun rule-makers. Mr McGee did not care for rules; he only cared about himself.

The factory started up its machines, and the Goblins worked with their little warty hands, mixed in with some Goblin magic, and out popped the shoes and boots. Hundreds of pairs came out of the factory and into the shops every day. Mr McGee's Magical Footwear was ready for people to buy, and the gold came pouring in! In no time at all, Mr McGee was rich.

People everywhere were buying McGee's magical shoes: 'floaters' to make the wearers float in the air, 'runners' to make the wearers run as fast as motor cars, and 'dancers' to make the wearers dance with grace no matter how flat-footed they were. But then things started to go very wrong.

Goblin magic is okay, but it's not as good as Leprechaun magic. Before long, dancing shoes began to float and floating shoes began to run and running shoes began to dance. Oh dear, what a mess!

Very soon, people became angry and wanted their money back. They were so angry they wrote letters of complaint to the Leprechaun rule-makers, who also became very angry. Mr McGee was in big trouble!

Soon afterwards, the Leprechaun police turned up at Mr McGee's factory and closed it down. They also took all of Mr McGee's gold and gave it back to the poor people who had bought his naughty shoes and boots, leaving Mr McGee penniless. Even his Goblin friends left him because they had not been paid.

Mr McGee sat on the steps of the empty factory and cried.

Then along came an old wizard called Will Whiskers. 'Why are you so sad, little man?' he asked.

Mr McGee told Will Whiskers the whole story about how he had tried to cheat and lie and break the rules; how it had only managed to make a mess and leave him alone with no money to buy food.

The old wizard listened to Mr McGee, and after the naughty Leprechaun had finished his tale, Will Whiskers reached into his bag and pulled out a purse full of gold.

'I have got money for food but no way of crossing the lake. I must get to the other side, and my old legs are too tired to walk around it. Maybe we can make a deal. I will pay you five gold coins for a pair of shoes that can walk on water. Can you make a pair like that?'

Mr McGee smiled. 'Easy-peasy,' he said as he popped off to his little Leprechaun house. 'Come and see me later. Your shoes will be ready!'

Later that day, Will Whiskers knocked on Mr McGee's door. 'Are my shoes ready?' he asked.

'They sure are!' the Leprechaun replied and handed the wizard the most beautiful pair of shoes, bright red with a lovely silver buckle.

Will Whiskers was very happy and handed Mr McGee five shiny gold coins. 'Well done, young man. They look wonderful! Now you can go and buy some food.' He tipped his large floppy hat and walked away, towards the lake.

That night, Mr McGee had a full belly and slept like a log, happy with his day's work.

The next morning, Mr McGee awoke to loud knocking on his door. *Oh no!* he thought. *I hope it's not more people complaining about my factory's shoes. I wish I had never broken the rules. I wish I had just been a good Leprechaun and done what I was told.*

Mr McGee walked to his front door and sheepishly opened it. To his surprise, he saw a long line of wizards, over twenty of them, all in a queue.

'Can I help you?' he asked.

'Yes, please,' they all said. 'Our friend Will Whiskers told us about the wonderful shoes you made him, and we all want a pair.'

Before he could say, 'Top of the morning!' all the wizards came forward and gave their orders: flying shoes, floating shoes, dancing shoes, running shoes, shoes to make you strong, shoes to help you swim, shoes that make no sound, even shoes to march up hills! Each wizard handed over five gold coins, and

Mr McGee was once again wealthy, but this time, he had done it all himself and broken no rules along the way.

The next year, Mr McGee married a lovely little Leprechauness called Naloo, and they had a little boy they called Hamish Jr. His daddy taught him all that he had learnt.

Cheating does not pay, but hard work always does. Mr McGee was not a naughty Leprechaun anymore. He was a very good one, and everyone wanted shoes made by McGee and Son's Magical Footwear.

CHAPTER 2

The Ill Tale of Slumber Vale

Spider was a horrid lad; of that there was no doubt,
always wanting his own way, or else he'd scream and shout.
Spider shouted rude, rude words at
people, dogs, and passing birds,
words to make a lemon curd, if a lemon could have heard.

Spider really didn't care. Spider cut off all his hair.
'Come and stop me if you dare!' with a nasty, chilling stare
behind a door or rocking chair, jumping out to cause a scare.
Naughty here, naughty there, Spider was a true nightmare.

He loved to make his neighbours mad; he
loved to make his mamma sad,
a naughty child of malcontent, anything but heaven sent.
Practical jokes, wicked hoax on unsuspecting, quiet folks,
everyone so full of dread, just like flies caught in his web.

This simply could not carry on; something surely must be done.
Before the time became too late and Spider sealed his grisly fate,
before they burnt him at the stake,
drastic measures they must take.
A daunting task, make no mistake; it
must be done for Spider's sake.

Spider marched towards the town,
upon his face the usual frown.
Plotting mischief in his mind, someone
to torment he must find.
So engrossed in schemes and plots, the
empty town he noticed not.
Ahead, the widow-woman stood, all
forlorn on a bridge of wood.

'Oh look! An old woman! Out alone! I'll scare
her to death with a ghostly moan!'
Then out of his mouth came a ghoulish tone,
to send a shiver through flesh and bone.
Spider waited for her to yell, but
instead, she rang a rusty bell.
The moon emerged from beyond the cloud;
the bell rang out both clear and loud.

Upon the bridge, the old hag cackled as
zombies passed her bound in shackles.
Spider froze in shock and fear as hordes
of bogeymen drew near.
Hellish ghouls and spooky fiends closed in
on Spider, who cried and screamed.
And in his panic, Spider fell, surrounded
by creatures straight out of Hell.
They ambled, and shuffled; some even crawled,
circling Spider curled up in a ball.

'Your wicked ways brought us back from the dead.
Now we've come for your soul!' the head zombie said.
'For every spiteful act you have done,
you must be punished! With us, you must come!'

'I'm sorry! I'm sorry. Oh, please let me be.
I can be good if you'll just set me free.
"That Spider is good!" they will say about me.
Return to the dark. I'll be nice; you will see.'

The undead converged and spoke of the child,
glancing at him every once in a while.
Spider remained in a heap on the floor.
Every second that passed made him cry even more.

He waited and prayed for the sun to appear
curled up in a huddle and puddle of tears,
trembling and shaking and riddled with fears,
eyes tightly shut and his hands on his ears.

'We've counselled together, and here is the plan …
We will grant you a chance, yes, to change if you can.
We will leave you this night, but at once will return
and take you down with us if you have not learnt.'

As dawn's first light spread across the small town,
he opened one eye, and he peered around,
then jumping with glee from his place on the ground.
To his joy and delight, not a ghoulie was found.

Now, if on your travels, you come to a town
where everyone's happy and no one is down,
you may find a lad conducting good deeds,
caring for people, and tending their needs.

He is jolly and friendly and laughs, and he sings.
The townsfolk, they love all the joy that he brings.
But when it is dark, and he lies in his bed,
he pulls all the covers up over his head.

He still has his nightmares; they keep him on track.
He's afraid that one night, all the ghouls will come back.
Although now his future is happy and bright,
he's afraid of the dark and afraid of the night.

So, don't be like Spider; be nice to all folk.
Be careful with teasing and practical jokes.
Remember his lesson: it came at a price.
Never be naughty, but choose to be nice.

To this day, it's a secret that few people tell—
how the townsfolk dressed up, yes, as ghoulies from Hell,
how they spent all the night by the bridge made of wood
to teach Spider a lesson and turn him to good.

CHAPTER 3

The Punishing of Loog

JARLANDY, A THRIVING TRADING TOWN IN THE WEST continent of Nogion, was home to the Blunderbear family. Loog Blunderbear was the son of a wealthy property owner and spoilt beyond repair by the age of three.

On his fifteenth birthday, Loog demanded a wizard to perform magic at his birthday party. Hiring a wizard for this purpose was not an easy task since the Blunderbear family had already employed most of the respectable wizards to entertain little Loog on each of his birthdays, and they had all met the same fate. Whenever a wizard cast a spell, it would go horribly wrong, much to the amusement of Loog. It seemed the horrid child possessed magic of his own. Over the years, party guests had been turned into all manner of beings, and animals turned into all manner of household items, such as egg whisks and whistles and cooking pans. The worse it got, the more amused Loog became.

So, for this occasion, Loog's father was forced to look outside of Jarlandy for a new wizard. This also proved an almost impossible task as word had spread among the Order of Wizards that little Loog Blunderbear was to be avoided like the plague.

On the night before his party, Loog Blunderbear the Third finally got his traditional performing wizard. In the caves bowing under the rock of Kraag, his father's messengers had found Mol-Ni-Akk, a yet unheard-of sorcerer.

The party was full of wealthy and important people, all of whom were wondering which wizard would be foolish or desperate enough to lend their services in honour of naughty, spoilt little Loog. At the stroke of nine, the fanfare sounded, and the party's host, Loog's uncle Vinston, announced the start of the night's magical extravaganza. There was a drum roll, and then the mysterious Mol-Ni-Akk entered the hall.

All inside the hall
heard the wizard's call.
As he entered to their right,
they beheld an awesome sight.

His hair black as pitch,
his cape of gems rich,
his face deathly white,
he gave them quite a fright.

His lips began to move
as he turned around to Loog.
Raising his arms high,
he let fly a wicked cry.

The children shrieked and ran.

Just imagine if you can,

like insects under stone,

all the people running home.

The women held their hems

as they hid behind the men.

The men sped for the door;

some were crawling on the floor.

A panic struck them down,

panic stricken to the ground,

at the ghastly, hellish sound

they could hear from all around.

As the wizard cast his spell,

Loog began to feel unwell.

Then dropping to his knees,

he shouted, 'Help me, Poppa, please.'

But Poppa wasn't there;

he was hid behind a chair,

full of panic and despair

like a rabbit in a snare.

Loog began to shake and shiver,
tears flowing like a river,
his whole body quite a quiver
from his eyeballs to his liver.

Then his limbs began to shrivel
as he turned a shade of purple;
for the lesson he must learn,
he was turned into a worm.

CHAPTER 4

A Rainy Night

WISHABELLE ANNOD WAS A GARDEN FAIRY, AND as is the case with all garden fairies, she lived to care for flowers, shrubs, and all things that grow. Garden fairies are attracted by well-kept gardens and love to make their homes in them.

A normal day for a garden fairy would be fighting off pests like green flies, wasps, and slugs. They use special fairy dust to help things grow; they also use their little magic wands to beat back weeds and brambles.

The hardest part of their day is warding off birds. Birds love to dig for worms and make a mess when they do so. This keeps garden fairies very busy indeed. Birds are beautiful, and Wishabelle loved them all, especially blackbirds, which sing the most wonderful songs. But boy oh boy, do they make a mess.

Rats, mice, shrews, and voles all stay away from gardens

tended by garden fairies, as they don't like being zapped with fairy magic.

Wishabelle lived in a beautiful little garden attached to the home of a lovely family called the Spantons. There were Mr and Mrs Spanton and their charming children: a little boy named Connor and his younger sister, Carla.

As is the way with most little girls, Carla loved dolls. She had dozens of them, too many for her to count with ease, all kinds of dolls from all kinds of places. Carla had learnt to expect a new addition to her collection every time a relative took a holiday. She would often wonder just how many countries there were in the world, and should she receive a doll from every country, where on earth would she put them all?

Carla loved all her dolls, but one thing about much-loved dolls is that the more they are played with, the more they become threadbare and ragged, disjointed and limp. The little girl knew that many of her beloved dolls were broken and was sad as a result, yet she loved them so dearly she could not bear to throw them away.

Carla slept deeply the night Wishabelle flew through her open window to escape the rain outside. The fairy had seen Carla at play and knew the girl was sweet and good, so the fairy decided to reward the little girl.

Wishabelle noticed the basket of broken dolls and immediately knew what she would do. One by one, the fairy silently removed the tattered dolls and placed them neatly on the bedroom floor, side by side in two rows. Then she took what she knew to be each doll's most lovable parts and magically mixed them up until all the bits were used. Wishabelle the fairy was pleased with her work and admired it for a moment before returning to the now rain-free garden.

When Carla awoke the following morning, she rubbed her sleepy eyes, sat upright, and yawned. It was then that she first saw them, and instantly, she felt she knew them; there in front of her were three new dolls of great splendour. She smiled as she recognized the parts of them she already loved so dearly, and she embraced them and held them and loved them and knew beyond a doubt that they loved her too.

CHAPTER 5

The Bad Boys of Bog Town

ONCE UPON A TIME, BROTHERS GOMER AND SPAMA were the bad boys of Bog Town, a little hamlet on the east side of the Weeping Woods. Gomer and Spama were notorious villains. However, they lacked the intelligence to get away with any of their ludicrous schemes. They robbed, lied, hustled, and harassed all day every day, but more often than not, they were caught. Finally, they were banished and forced to roam the land in search of their skulduggery.

A witch doesn't always look like a witch, and this was certainly the case with the witch the brothers tried to con out of her cow. The witch in this case was a beautiful, golden-haired maiden who kept a small farm and herb garden just inside the forest boundaries.

Her appearance was so not witchlike that the brothers thought she would be easy prey for their ploys. And so they tried to convince her that they were talent scouts looking for worthy animals to enter into the National Farmers' Fair to be held that week. The brothers went on to tell her that the winning animal's owner would receive one hundred gold pieces as a prize and that her cow was top quality and would surely win.

The witch smiled and nodded as the pair wove their web of lies. They suggested that they should take the cow to be weighed and measured, ready for the big event, at which she was to be a VIP guest.

As the brothers led the cow down the path away from the witch's farm, they waved at the witch whilst smiling and shouting, 'See you on Thursday, good lady! We will have this beast looking tip-top.' They hurried along the path as the witch simply stood there smiling and waving back at them.

The sun shone and the birds tweeted in the trees as the pair approached the gate of the farm. Oh, the excitement and sense of delight! One of their plans had actually worked!

'I can taste the steak and chips already!' Gomer muttered out of the side of his mouth to his chuckling brother.

'I told you this would work!' Spama replied as the two pressed on with ever-quicker steps.

Suddenly, a wind began to rise, and the sky seemed to darken.

Strength mysteriously left the brothers' legs, and they fell to the ground as if dead. They began whimpering and crying.

Then they heard the witch's voice, and with it, her curse:

Sheep, pigs, and cows I keep,

and water from a well so deep.

Herbs and potions on my shelf,

a life of peace I made myself.

Upon my door, you boldly rapped

to trick and swindle, snare and trap.

But not this day will trouble win;

upon your heads, your tricks will spin.

You saw me as an easy prey,
to feed on me—but not today!
You see yourselves as clever beasts;
upon my cow, you wished to feast.

If beasts you think yourselves to be,
this gift I give to you for free.
Hiding your nature is so unfair,
so now become a wolf and bear!

Your bellies always wanting more,
your skin will itch and make you sore;
your matted fur a home for fleas,
a wretched sight for all to see.

So, in this form, you both shall roam,
these woods forever your new home.
Forever tread these woodland tracts,
until your hearts will melt like wax.

And so, our tale comes to an end; now tell it to your kin
and friends.
Let all be warned, let all beware, lest
they become a wolf or bear.

Be honest, good, and do no wrong, and you will live both

well and long.

Be kind to all, both poor and rich—

you never know who is a witch.

CHAPTER 6

Those of Nogion

The Grotchit

I love to sit and watch it, this thing they call a Grotchit.
It leaps and whirls around, yet hardly makes a sound.
Its legs are fat and strong; its arms are thin and long.
Its eyes, like bugs, are big. It wears a purple wig.

And as I sit and watch it, I clap and praise the Grotchit.
Such fun it seems to have, never glum or sad.
It cares not what I think, its body round and pink.
It smiles and laughs away, cares not what others say.

Such joy it is to watch it, this happy thing a Grotchit.
It has no worries, has no fears, content with both its floppy ears.
It dances round and strikes a pose, then
trumpets from its yellow nose.
Ponders not on wins or fails, parading round with fluffy tails.

My pleasure is to watch it, this thing they call a Grotchit.

It really is a treat, wears slippers on its feet.

Frolics why? For what? For who?

Around its waist a pink tutu.

I hope one day that I will be just like

the Grotchit, worry-free.

The Kronk

We will call it a 'he' instead of a 'she',
although it is neither, as soon you will see.
Blobby in texture and blobby to touch,
that is why people don't hug him so much.

All over his body are round orange spots,
too big not to notice, too large to call dots.
There on his head, on a stalk is his eye;
he can't wear a hat, but he sure can spy.

His feet are like saucers, both round and both flat;
on both of his shoulders are wings like a bat.
A tail like a snail and ears like a vole,
with claws on his fingers like those of a mole.

Inside of his mouth hang a row of white teeth,
but the teeth underneath are as green as a leaf.
And now I suppose I will speak of his nose,
just as thick as a brick and as red as a rose.

I should also mention another small thing:
each of his fingers are eight golden rings.
The rings they are furnished with pearls from the sea;
if you ask him politely, he will give one for free.

He eats figs and berries and drinks morning dew,
gathers them up and makes fig berry stew.
On Mondays, he marches a mile and a half,
tells jokes to himself, and has a good laugh.

A peculiar creature, yes, one of a kind,
but more mellow a fellow you never will find.
Spends most of his day fast asleep in a tree,
and the rest of the time, he sings songs and drinks tea.

Where is the Kronk from? It's a mystery still.
From over a mountain? Or under a hill?
Maybe the Kronk knows from where he first came,
or maybe he doesn't and wonders the same.

Gob-O-lins

Few are more misunderstood;
indeed, if creatures ever could.
Few get a ride that's rougher
than Gob-O-lins disliked by others.

Folks do flee; that's no surprise,
With warty skin and weird eyes,
Pointy ears green like leaves,
Smelly breath, and knobbly knees.

No wonder people up and run,
Like bullets from a smoking gun.
When Gob-O-lins walk in the room,
The air is filled with doom and gloom.

They mean no harm; they mean no ill.
To make you squirm is not their will.
Although their voices rasp and wheeze,
They are polite and aim to please.

When underneath, you care to look,
You'll read them like an open book.
They work so hard and help the needy.
Not asking much, they are not greedy.

If Gob-O-lins walk up to you,
Say, 'Hey, hello, how do you do?'
Treat them well, and make a friend,
They'll stick with you until the end.

A Gunnyding

What a thing a Gunnyding,
Voice like birds, they love to sing.
Arms most big, made to dig,
Friend to rock and leaf and twig.

What a thing a Gunnyding,
Worker for the dragon king.
Home a hole, filled with coal,
Sees in the dark, just like a mole.

What a thing a Gunnyding,
Bouncy like a shiny spring.
Full of fun, full of joy,
Playful like a child's toy.

What a thing a Gunnyding,
In each ear a golden ring.
Working boots that suit them fine,
Helping folk who dig in mines.

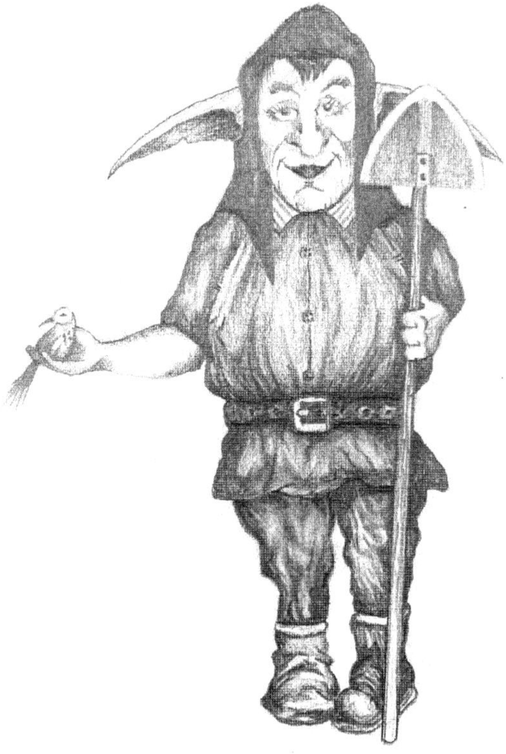

Wizards

Do they all wear floppy hats?
Do they all eat toads and bats?
Do they all have lengthy beards?
Do they all look oh so weird?

Wizards, wizards, mysterious wizards
Controlling the weather with lightning and blizzards.
Wizards, wizards, mysterious wizards
Roaming the land over hills, plains, and rivers.

Do they all have magic powers?
Do they all read books for hours?
Do they all walk miles and miles?
Do they all have charming smiles?

Wizards, wizards, mysterious wizards
Turning their foes into snakes, goats, and lizards.
Wizards, wizards, mysterious wizards
Casting their spells with words sharp as scissors.

Yes, they all wear floppy hats.
Yes, they all eat toads and bats.
Yes, they all have lengthy beards.
Yes, they all look oh so weird.

Yes, they all have magic powers.

Yes, they all read books, for hours.

Yes, they all walk miles and miles.

Yes, they all have charming smiles.

Wizards.

CHAPTER 7

China Cats and Coal Mines

CHRISTIAN TIPTOED INTO THE DIM HALLWAY OF the small terraced house. The first thing he noticed was the smell, an odour that can only be found in elderly people's homes—a kind of stale smell, but not, however, an unpleasant one. In fact, the boy found something about it comforting.

Mounted on the left-hand wall was a glass telephone shelf. Beside the telephone sat a life-size ornamental Siamese cat with piercing blue eyes.

The cat seemed to be staring at him under its brow. Christian shivered but could not peel his eyes from it. If it were not for the shiny glaze, he would have sworn the china cat had a pulse. He slowly reached out his right hand, half expecting the cat to hiss or snarl or maybe even take a swipe at him, when suddenly the door directly in front of Christian flew open, and a round-faced figure rushed in.

'Did I scare you, Smiler?' It was only Pat. She was always calling Christian Smiler because he remained a happy lad even in the worst of times.

'I'm serious,' she said. 'You look like you've seen a ghost!' Pat felt the boy's forehead, just like he guessed she would. She never stopped fussing over Christian's well-being. He knew she had reason to worry, too. Pat Holt was Christian's guardian, and because of the misfortunes the boy had suffered, she was especially protective of him. Christian's mother had passed away the very morning he was born. His father had died six years later in an industrial accident. So, Christian had been taken in by Pat, who had been the lifelong friend of his late mother.

It so happened that Pat's father was an old coal miner who still lived in the same terraced house in Cwmgors that Pat had been raised in. The man was in poor health these days, and Pat had to call on him no less than twice a day. This morning, she was taking Christian into Swansea to pick up some new summer clothes. Christian had had a growing spurt of late, and none of his old shorts and T-shirts fitted him anymore.

On the way, Pat and Christian stopped by Pat's dad's house so she could tend to the old miner. Pat had never taken Christian to meet her elderly father. She had considered the matter carefully before finally deciding that she would not introduce the pair since the old miner was so very ill. She dared not expose the young boy to unnecessary heartache.

Poor Christian might grow very fond of her father, only to lose him as he had his parents.

It had been five years since Pat made that decision, and the old miner had surpassed all expectations as to how long he might live. Now the lad was older and had expressed his desire to meet Pat's dad after overhearing a conversation between Pat and her auntie Kathleen. He had heard Pat say, 'Any day now, Auntie Kathy. They say his brain is shutting down.' Christian found this comment shocking and was saddened to his core. His intuitive mind grasped the inevitability that the old man's brain was switching off. It meant, of course, that he was dying, and this made Christian feel that he wanted to see Pat's dad before it was too late. He wanted to meet the man he had heard so many stories about.

Christian had a mental image of the man, and now he wondered if his imagination was anywhere near the mark. He was sure it was not. The stories he had heard from Pat were of days when the miner would swing his little girl around and around above his head as the pair would laugh and laugh; of days when she would ride around the coffee table on her daddy's back with a feather in her hair as father and daughter played Cowgirls and Indians. Christian guessed that the old miner's cowboy days were sadly at an end.

'I've made him some toast,' Pat said. She looked even kinder in the dim light of the old hallway. 'Not that he will eat it, mind you. He just sucks the butter off, lately. They say, "Old age cometh not alone", and it's true, Smiler.' She balanced the laden tray across her left forearm and reached for the living-room door's handle. 'Now I'll just be a couple minutes,' she whispered.

As she cracked the creaking door open, a peculiar low light flickered from the silent room, and she slipped inside.

Christian poked in his head. The TV alone illuminated the space, crowded with very old furniture and strange black-and-white pictures on the walls. On the TV screen, a crazy-looking heavy-metal band with scrunched-up faces and wild hair thrashed away at their guitars and drums, looking like a mime act from Hell. Christian was glad the volume was turned off. In fact, the only sound coming from the room was the metronomic timing of a concealed carriage clock.

In the shadowy corner was the silhouette of a seated figure. Christian could make out a tartan blanket neatly covering a pair of seemingly withered legs, lit by the strobe-like effect of the television. The sleeping man appeared elderly and somewhat gaunt of face. In the eerie light of the TV, his sunken eyes cast long shadows over square cheeks. Pat made her way over to the old man in the corner. Then she seemed to remember something and turned around to see Christian peering in.

'I need to close the door, love; the light hurts his eyes,' Pat whispered. 'I don't mean to be rude.' She winked at him and softly shut the door behind her.

Christian stood alone in the hall and checked his watch—22.22 pm it flashed. He huffed in bafflement. Impatiently tapping the tiny buttons on the watch, he attempted to return it to the correct setting. But it continued to read 22.22 pm.

'It's the morning, not the evening, you stupid watch!' Christian whined as he battled with the buttons.

The door flew open. Christian jumped in fright again as Pat emerged from the gloom still holding the tray with its untouched contents.

'I'll be back in five minutes, love,' she said as she hurried past him and out the front door.

Pat seems rather scatterbrained today, Christian thought.

'And who might you be?' came a rasping voice from within the darkness of the living room.

Christian turned to see the seated figure looking directly at him, though the face no longer carried the gaunt mask of age. Instead, the man resembled Pat in both roundness and kindness of face.

'Come in, lad. Let me take a look at you.'

Christian crept into the purple shadows. Then, to his

surprise, he could not help but smile back into the kind old eyes that met him.

'Now let me guess—you look like an Ian,' the man said. 'No wait! Maybe not. Maybe more like a Chris, or maybe you're both. Maybe you're a Chris-t-Ian.'

Christian paused in thought, then chirped, 'Pat must have told you my name!'

The man leaned forward. He had the calming scent of pipe tobacco about him. 'Maybe she did, maybe she didn't. To be honest, I can't quite remember myself. It's my marbles, you see. They say I've lost them. Mind you, they have been telling me that since I was about your age. How old are you, bach?'

'I am twelve, nearly thirteen, sir,' Christian said.

'Call me Sam, bach. I never could stand being called *sir*. It just don't sit right.'

The boy shifted back and forth on the balls of his feet. He wondered how much to ask of this elderly gent nestled away in this quiet, old house.

'What happened when you were my age, Sam?'

'When I was your age?' The old man's face wrenched in confusion.

'You said they have been telling you that you lost your marbles since you were about my age,' the boy practically whispered, so as not to alarm him. 'What happened, Sam?'

Suddenly, the old man's eyes lit up. 'Oh, right, yes. I'm with you now. When I was your age—I remember like it was yesterday.' Sam paused and rubbed his bristly chin. Then he looked sharply at Christian and asked in a mysterious tone, 'Do you still believe in magic, Christian?'

'Magic?'

'Yes ... MAGIC!'

'Not really sure,' Christian said. But what he really wasn't sure about was the old man's sanity. 'I don't suppose so. Not real magic, anyway. My uncle Mortimer—well, he's my step-uncle really—he does some brilliant tricks. But that's not real magic, is it?'

The man smiled kindly at Christian. 'Magic is when

something unbelievable happens, when something occurs that has no rational explanation. What's the best trick your uncle does, bach?'

Christian thought for a moment. 'Probably his disappearing spoon trick.'

'Oh, that sounds interesting.' The old man shifted forward in his chair and grunted with a bit of difficulty. 'Do you know how he does it?'

'Now I do, but for ages, he had me guessing.'

'So, until you saw how it was done, you thought it was magic.'

'Yes.' Christian felt a slight draft. There seemed to be just a wee bit more light in the room now.

'So, do you think magic is real until we can explain it?' the old man went on.

That was a stumper. Christian began searching his thoughts.

'Sit down, boy. It's hurting my old neck looking up at you.'

The boy looked to the right of Sam and saw a small stool. He took it. 'I'm not sure, Sam,' Christian said. 'What made you bring up the subject of magic, anyway?'

'Ah!' said Sam, as if wind had suddenly filled his sails. 'And I thought you were never going to ask!' He leaned back in the chair, settling in for a trip back in time.

'When I was a little older than you, I was already working at the mine. Me and my uncle were working the face. The picks were flying and the coal was falling. We used to dig it by hand in them days, and hard graft it was too, boy.

'I remember once when I stopped to wipe my brow and looked up, I noticed one of the supporting beams above our heads was bowing, so I called my uncle Shinkin and pointed it out to him. He said I had done well to spot it, and he went to tell the boss. I could see them talking and pointing from down the tunnel. Then my uncle started to make his way back up to me. I asked him what was going on, and he told me that a timber gang would be there right away to fix it. So, we had a spell sitting on the floor, chatting away as me and my uncle Shinks liked to do. I reached into my pocket and pulled out a jam sandwich wrapped in paper. I broke it in half and gave some to my uncle. I can still taste the strawberries now, handmade jam from Mamgi Shop. Oh, it was out of this world!'

Christian could practically taste the jam just from the way Sam's voice rose and fell in excitement.

'Then Shinks started to tell me a story about how my father and he had been caught pinching strawberries from Mamgi Shop's field down the Gower. Well, halfway through the story, the wooden beam above our heads started to creak and groan, and the next thing I knew, we were plunged into total darkness. The beam had collapsed under the weight of the coal above. There was coal dust everywhere—in my mouth, in my eyes. Pitch black. I couldn't breathe for the dust.

"'Shinkin, Shinkin,' I called between coughs and gasps. "Where are you, Uncle?" I was petrified, searching the air and the ground, frantically calling for my uncle. "Shinkin, Shinkin, where are you? I'm scared, I'm scared." But no answer came. Then my hands found a boot, then a leg, then a wooden beam lying across my poor uncle's back. "Wake up, Uncle. It's Sammy," I cried. "Wake up, Shinks. I need you. Don't be dead. Please don't be dead.'"

Christian felt his lip tremble. He tried not to think of his father.

'Then I started to say something—something I had completely forgotten I even knew! It was an old nursery rhyme my uncle had taught me when I was no taller than Tubby, our dog. For years and years, miners have told tales of fairy folk who live in the mines—friends to the Welsh miners. Some call them the knockers; others call them the Gunnydings. There was an old nursery rhyme about them, and it went like this:

If down the pit you dare to go,
the only light a lantern's glow.
Where Welshmen dig and mine for coal,
deep within a pitch-black hole.

If you're scared and can't get out,
these magic words be sure to shout:
'Help me! Help me! Gunnydings,
hear this dafty digger sing.
Lead me out into the light
out of this hole, as black as night.'

'Over and over, I cried, "Help me! Help me, Gunnydings. Help me!" Over and over and over. "Help me, help me, Gunnydings!" I was desperately trying to lift the beam off of my poor uncle's back, but it just wouldn't move. The tears were flowing down my cheeks, mixing with the coal dust. I collapsed onto the beam, weeping uncontrollably, when I was suddenly aware of a dim blue light. It seemed to be coming from behind me. I looked around and saw something that I couldn't believe I was seeing. Something that should not have been there. Something that was no less than magical.'

At that, the old man seemed to be lost in his own memory.

'What was there?' Christian asked, practically tipping off his stool.

'A Gunnyding.'

'A whaty-ding? What's that word?'

'Not a whaty-ding, a Gunnyding,' said Sam.

Christian shook his head. 'But I don't know what a Gunnyding is. Sorry, Sam.'

'Well, you wouldn't, bach.' Sam's eyes were now as clear and bright as a baby's. 'At that time, neither did I. To me, a Gunnyding was nothing more than a character from a nonsensical old nursery rhyme. Yet there I was, looking at a small, luminous creature with arms and legs like yours and mine, with a cheerful face and pointy ears. He was wearing a waistcoat and boots, a sackcloth cap, and shorts that finished just above his knees. I checked my head for cuts and bumps, thinking I must be suffering from a knock to the head and hallucinating—that kind of thing. But there were no cuts and no bumps. I hadn't been hit on the head, and I wasn't hallucinating.'

'What happened then, Sam?' Christian asked. He could feel his heart beating faster.

'Well, I asked him who he was!'

'Did he answer you?'

'Oh yes! In a comical little voice, he replied, "I'm called Mooki, and I am here to help. Now, don't worry; out into light we go.' Then he disappeared for a few seconds before reappearing on my right. 'Dicky-dokes, righty-right, back in sight,' said Mooki before bending down and picking up a piece of coal. I watched in amazement as the piece of coal turned into a shiny diamond. Then the Gunnyding walked over to the coal face and drew a big circle with the diamond, which lit up to show a ring of burning fire. Taking two steps backward, he turned to me and winked. "He-he, ready for a surprise?" he said, chuckling. I just nodded continually, not believing what I was seeing. Well, would you?'

Christian shook his head. 'What was the surprise?'

'The surprise was this. He ran up to the coal face and kicked it.'

'What? That's it?' Christian fell back on his stool.

'I thought so,' said Sam. 'But then, where the Gunnyding had drawn the circle, a round hole appeared, flooding the mineshaft with daylight, blinding me for a moment. I covered my eyes, and then when I opened them again, the Gunnyding was—'

'GONE!' Christian shouted. He had almost forgotten— this wasn't storytelling hour at school.

'No, he was still there,' said Sam. '"Out you go, dafty digger. Remember not to dig downside up. Always dig left to right and never upside down," said the Gunnyding, still chuckling when he really did disappear. Well, I heard something hit the ground. I looked down and saw a huge diamond. I picked it up and walked out of the pit into the daylight and then heard a voice say, "Don't forget friendly Gunnydings." I turned around, expecting to see Mooki the Gunnyding standing there.'

'Was he there?' Christian asked.

'No, he wasn't,' Sam said, staring pensively into the amethyst murk of the cramped room. 'And neither was the hole. Instead, there were trees and grass and ground. I was in the woodland west of the mine. They couldn't explain how I got there or where the diamond came from. And when they found my poor uncle Shinkin, the timber had been lifted off his back, and he was still alive, although he spent the rest of his days thereafter in a wheelchair.'

A thoughtful silence descended upon the two for a moment.

'Did your uncle see the Gunnyding?' the boy asked.

'No.' Sam sighed. 'Old Shinks remembered nothing after the jam sandwich. But he believed me when I told him about Mooki the Gunnyding. Everyone else thought I was suffering from some sort of stress and my mind had invented the Gunnyding to help me to find a way out.'

Christian heard a sad weariness in the old man's voice. 'And what happened to the diamond, Sam? Did you sell it?'

A glimmer came to the old man's eye. Christian waited patiently as Sam fumbled down the side of his chair and then offered his hand. Christian slowly reached out to meet Sam's hand, and he dropped a shiny diamond into the boy's upturned palm. The muted colours of the TV sparkled through the gem. Christian watched the rich pageant of light at play in each angle. He knew right then he had never ever seen anything quite so sublime.

'Keep it, my boy,' Sam said with a smile.

'No way. I couldn't!' The boy was certain the old miner had gotten carried away, and would regret his offer.

'You could, and you should.' Sam winked at him. 'Pippin thinks you should have it.'

'Pippin?' said Christian.

'Ah yes, Pippin the cat.' Sam pointed to the fireplace. There on the mantelpiece was an exact replica of the lifelike ornamental cat in the hallway.

'Oh, you've got a pair of them,' Christian said. Every time he saw one of those things, he felt a cold tingle in his chest.

'No, there's just the one.'

The boy realized his new friend must be confused. 'No, I saw one in the hallway. It was exactly the same.'

'Oh yes, of course.' The old man chuckled. 'No, there's only the one Pippin. He just likes to move around a bit.' He smiled and again leaned in close. 'The thing is, bach, once you've been touched by magic, it kind of stays with you,' he said as he gave Christian a warm pat on the shoulder.

'But I saw it out there!'

Christian shot up from the stool and went to the doorway and out into the dim hall. He stopped in shock. The glass telephone shelf where the cat had been was now empty.

'It's gone,' Christian said, rubbing his forehead. 'It's not there. But that's impossible!' Then he noticed Sam had fallen asleep again, just as he could hear Pat's feet coming up the steps. 'Pat, Pat, quick!' he shouted.

Pat entered the hallway with a melancholy look on her face and walked over to Christian, tenderly taking his cheeks into the palms of her hands. 'Shhh, Smiler. Hush now, don't be scared.'

'But, but ...' Christian stammered.

'Now, now, bach, we all have to go someday. It was his time; that's all.'

Christian stared at her in bewilderment. 'What do you mean, Pat?'

'He was very old and had a good life,' she said. 'He's at peace now.' Christian felt a lump in his throat. She couldn't mean that Sam was dead, could she?

'I should have told you before I ran over to Enid.' A tear ran down Pat's cheek. 'When I took his breakfast in, I called his name, but he didn't answer, and when I checked him, I found his breathing was so very faint. Then he just passed away, at twenty-two minutes past ten.'

Christian's mind raced. 'But that means he died before ...' He gulped hard as he realized something very strange had just happened to him. He opened his hand only to find the diamond was no longer there. Instead, there was a piece of coal as black as pitch! In the midst of his shock, Christian had the unsettling sensation he was being watched.

And there, back on the telephone shelf, sat Pippin, the china Siamese cat.

To be continued in ...

The Last of the Gunnydings

ABOUT THE AUTHOR

David Morgan grew up in a house full of stories. Some of his earliest memories are of the Morgan household sitting around the table sharing stories, both true and tall. The family's love for movies, books, comics and television further fuelled his passion for storytelling. When the family wasn't reading stories, listening to stories or telling stories, they were drawing, painting or writing stories. At 12 years of age, David produced his very own comic book which proved to be a big hit with his classmates. His 'yarn spinning' continued into adulthood and when his two daughters came along, David found his ready audience.

Through the many phases of David's life – as a welder, a bouncer, a salesman, a karate instructor and a stand-up comedian, also, sadly, experiencing and overcoming the challenges of addiction and homelessness, his passion for creating stories and his strong faith in God have endured.

Today, David and his ever-supportive wife Emma, pastor a thriving Church in his hometown of Swansea, South Wales, where he brings his many life experiences and moral learning curves into his preaching and storytelling.

.

Lightning Source UK Ltd.
Milton Keynes UK
UKHW010000171221
395803UK00002B/46